"In a rapturous fusion of myth, imagination, philosophy, and human history, *Dreamlives of Debris* delivers us to the pure poetry of perception. I fell in love with *Debris*. Monstrous in form, radiant in spirit, she hears everyone: Sappho, Sophocles, Borges, Plato, a traveler on the Silk Road, Danielle Steele. Brigitte Reimann grieves her own diminishment as Bradley Manning explains his transition to Chelsea. No words seem more profound or true than any other. Those who dare to listen this way will be transfigured, scattered through time and space, bewildered, ecstatically alive, forever lost in a vast labyrinth of infinite possibilities."

—MELANIE RAE THON, AUTHOR OF *VOICE OF THE RIVER, SILENCE & SONG*, AND *THE 7TH MAN*

"Breaking boundaries of horror, science fiction, nonfiction, love story, and myth, this rare and brilliant novel reinvents the female 'monster' in the form of a disfigured girl. Subverting the hero's journey, *Debris* goes on a quest to find her self within an impossible labyrinth where architecture mirrors the disfigured female body, imprisoning and revealing a girl monster who stands between humanity and the darkness. In this world where what seems to be monstrous is more human than human, the stories most difficult to tell are the ones we most need to be told."

—AIMEE PARKISON, AUTHOR OF *REFRIGERATED MUSIC FOR A GLEAMING WOMAN*

dreamlives *of* debris

dreamlives *of* debris

lance olsen

DZANC
BOOKS

DZANC BOOKS

5220 Dexter Ann Arbor Rd.
Ann Arbor, MI 48103
www.dzancbooks.org

First US edition: April 2017

ISBN: 978-1-938604-58-4

Library of Congress Cataloging-in-Publication Data

Names: Olsen, Lance, 1956- author.Title: Dreamlives of debris / Lance Olsen.Description: Ann Arbor, MI : Dzanc Books, 2017.Identifiers: LCCN 2016034361 | ISBN 9781938604584 (paperback)Subjects: | BISAC: FICTION / Literary. | GSAFD: Fantasy fiction.Classification: LCC PS3565.L777 D74 2017 | DDC 813/.54--dc23LC record available at https://lccn.loc.gov/2016034361

Printed in the United States of America

10   9   8   7   6   5   4   3   2   1

acknowledgments

Huge thanks to *Conjunctions*, *Literature of Our Climes*, and *Rampike*, in which excerpts from this book first appeared in slightly different form; the Deutscher Akademischer Austauschdienst Berliner Künstlerprogramm for giving me time, space, and support to complete this project; the University Research Committee & Creative Grant and International Travel and Research Grant from the University of Utah for enabling me to visit various archeological sites and museums around Crete; and Steve Halle for talking me through some of the niceties of InDesign.

for Andi, without whom nothing would ever make sense

how to lose your breath : foreword

Breathtaking.

There are very few books around lately that I find breathtaking. I mean books that happen to me such that I hold my breath while reading them, or more, books that take my breath from me so that breath travels, giving life to language and then returning to me as if to remind me that I, too, am alive, differently than before.

I mean the place and time called language.

I mean before the after of language, when meanings suture shut.

Language that can happen to you.

Lance Olsen's *Dreamlives of Debris* takes us back to some of our earliest meaning-making mythologies, specifically disfiguring and refiguring the Theseus and Minotaur myths. However, instead of the Minotaur being a half-bull/half-man monster, she's a little deformed girl through which voices from the future speak.

You could say that I am an ideal reader for this book.

Beyond ideal.

Deep into the prehistory imaginal.

I'll tell you why later.

One of my biggest beefs with our inherited histories and mythologies is that, on the one hand, they went from an oral tradition made of voice to "authored," you know, written, and thus they seem mysteriously locked and located by mono interpretations. This has always seemed idiotic to me, considering that the definitions of myth we operate within contain within them their own contradictions:

Myth :: noun

1. a traditional or legendary story, usually concerning some being or hero or event, with or without a determinable basis of fact or a natural explanation, especially one that is concerned with deities or demigods and explains some practice, rite, or phenomenon of nature.

2. stories or matter of this kind:

realm of myth.

3. any invented story, idea, or concept:

His account of the event is pure myth.

4. an imaginary or fictitious thing or person.

5. an unproved or false collective belief that is used to justify a social institution.

I've always suspected the mono interpretations of our inherited myths serve to give some people and not others power, celebrity, jobs, titles, expertise, careers. At best. At worst, sanctioned and anointed mono meanings legitimize certain bodies, voices, and experiences and not others. For very long periods of time. Tortuously long for those bodies and voices repressed and oppressed, those whose stories are subsumed by the dominant culture. Think of the Oedipus myth. Or the Christ story. Now think of all the bodies and voices erased, repressed, and oppressed by them.

That's why I like to think of myth as something we can go back to, disfigure, refigure by endlessly making art. By ignoring linear time (which is itself a fiction). I like to think of myth more like a palimpsest carrying the trace of former meanings even as new stories flex and surge.

What stole my breath while I was reading this book was the language and form first, as if a perfect poetics had been designed to give voice and body to the story of a girl monster remaking all prior myth, all prior history and philosophy of being and knowing, phenomenally. Her unusual body the word for it.

This is a story about what is lodged between language and silence, speech and sound, reality and the imagination: not the Christ body, not any other painstakingly constructed myth from which we built Western culture, but a body that we are a little afraid of. A body that doesn't fit the hero's journey. A body that never transcends time or place, but remains stubbornly and timelessly material. Grounded. The body of a deformed girl.

This is also the story of the labyrinth called language, where meaning could take any turn, or return, or "maze" us into a new "whirled."

At the center of the labyrinth, you will find a disfigured girl suffering all of our meaning-making acts at the level of her actual body and imagination. You will move through a multiplicity of fragmented voices and songs and stories, through history, philosophy, theologies, gods and demigods, but also through consumerism and the Internet and pop culture and art and war and love and hatred, all through the body and voice of a girl. Her body informed and thus deformed by our acts of interpretation.

Voices in the story will come from everywhere and yet return over and over again to one voice; her voice will be your only tether to what you "know." Your previous body of knowledge against the fact of her material body, present tense, or present made tense, speaking the futurepastnow. Your journey will be through the fragmentation and displacement of all meaning — dreamtime, dreamspace, dreamlives, dreamlanguages — emanating from the body of this irreducable deformed girl, unmaking Myth back into floating pieces of stories and things: words and bodies.

The girl, whose name is Debris (re-membering a kind of Benjaminian historical materialism by echoing "history as a pile of debris," a kind of hovering Angelus Novus her accompaniment), asks: "When did stories become so difficult to tell?" It's a question that haunts me about the book, but also about storymaking today. What we've made of ourselves. Our world. Our meanings.

My first child was born a girl. She died the day she was born. My mother was afraid to look at her, or hold her, or breathe. I held her, I loved her, I breathed her in. From her lifedeath, I learned to unmake and remake stories. Endlessly.

Follow this beautiful, disfigured girl named Debris.

Beginend with her breath and body, destoried and restoried.

Breathtakingly.

— Lidia Yuknavitch

Someone, I tell you, in another time will remember us, but never as who we were.

—SAPPHO

The sound
Of the horses like roses being burned alive.

— STESICHOROS

:::: **DEBRIS**

I have my doll and the screamings behind my eyes. The screamings look like fluttery lights. They believe they live inside me. I live inside them, too.

My doll's name is Catastrophe.

:::: **DEBRIS**

There was a day my daddy made his ideas purer than King Aegeus'. Now every year King Aegeus sends a yearning of his bravest young men and most beautiful young women from Athens to visit me. I let them wander the passages of my heart for hours — days — maybe weeks — I don't know what any of these words mean — before stepping out of their frothy panic to welcome them.

:::: **DEBRIS**

Apis the Healer tells me I am thirty-three years old. He tells me nobody thought I would live beyond my thirty-second. This is why Mommy calls me My Little Duration, why Daddy calls me Minotaur.

I call myself Debris.

:::: DEBRIS

I say once, say *now*, say *hours*, *days*, *weeks*, only I don't understand myself. Down here time is a storm-swarmed ship always shivering itself into pieces.

:::: DEBRIS

Sometimes I can't locate the walls. Maybe I should mention this. Maybe I already have. Maybe everything is everything and then I am shuffling forward, hands outstretched in the grainy charcoal air, inhaling mold, must, fungus, sulfur, red angels, damp dirt, wet rock, waiting for the gritty chafe ushering me onto the far shore.

:::: **DEBRIS**

Despite my height, my strength is not negligible.

Last month — no — I'm not sure — I'm never sure — one always knows a little less than one did a flinch ago — at some point in — look at me — I am trotting through my corridors — running — one could describe this motion as progress if one wished — at some point Mommy and Daddy gave me a little sister to play with.

Our embrace persisted the length of one short, startled bleat.

Since then I have been an only child again.

:::: **DEBRIS**

Sometimes so many walls erupt around me I am forced to
crab sideways to make any headway at all.

:::: DEBRIS

Mommy tells me Daddy's Little Duration is just like everybody else, only inside out. She is just like everybody else, only more so.

Meaning it was very bad to believe in belief.

Meaning it was very good to believe every idea had a shape.

Meaning when Apis the Healer last stood me against the measuring wall, he recorded a height of thirty-three inches, and when he last lifted me onto his golden scales, he recorded a weight of thirty-three pounds.

My head hogs more of that total than heads normally do.

This is why I am quicker than most.

:::: **DEBRIS**

When I set out to welcome my new guests — I am running
again — call this running — how did that happen? — when
I set out to welcome my new guests I tuck Catastrophe
under my arm — tuck my baby brother under my arm
and carry a torch — not so I can see them — no — but so
they can see me — when it counts — when we say hello
to each other — and the brave young men — the brave
young unarmed men usually shit themselves — shit or piss
themselves — as I step into the open — a not altogether
surprising sight — neither an altogether surprising nor an
altogether unamusing one — watching them blunder into
blank walls — watching that piss and shit trickling down
their ambitions.

:::: DEBRIS

My tiny ears poke up attentive as a Cretan hound's. This is why I can hear the past and future as well as the present.

:::: **DEBRIS**

Daedalus designed my heart. Maybe I should mention this. Maybe I already have. Finished, he could barely find his own way out.

His nomad mind lives in the bloodless body of a man-sized toad sans ass.

He wears the perpetual grimace of a Skeptic.

I have never seen him smile.

Not once.

Smiling for him is cataclysm.

His crimped gray face carries the same message wherever it goes: *Stand a little less between me and the darkness.*

:::: **DEBRIS**

Sometimes the ceiling sinks without warning and then I am crawling on my belly through the paradox, baby brother clutched tight to my chest.

:::: **DEBRIS**

Sometimes the walls become a whirlwind of hands or dying alphabets.

:::: DEBRIS

Sometimes, torchless, baby-brotherless, I follow my
gift women like their own shadows. They can't hear
me, possess no sense of my presence, until they feel me
clambering up their backs, hands searching out necks,
reckless teeth arteries.

::::: DEBRIS

What I am telling you, I want to say, is a love story.

::::: DEBRIS

Let us call what I am telling you a love story.

::: DEBRIS

Let us say my eyes are the color of polished onyx.

::: DEBRIS

Let us say my skin —

:::: DEBRIS

— my skin is so thin you can see lavender flatworms quivering beneath it like quick little ideas, and sometimes I wake alarmed from a dreamless sleep din, world all black rabbit snifts among my ribs, wondering if everyone has finally forgotten me. It is not unimaginable. It is not unimaginable and it is. I am borrowed eyes, borrowed ears, borrowed tongue. How long has it been since Mommy rocked Her Little Duration? Since the eunuch priests loosed one of their pigs ruffling with sacrificial ribbons to snort through my heart? Since they hid an amphora teeming with lily tastes, rose tastes, the tastes interesting injuries, a new toy for me to treasure out?

:::: **DEBRIS**

And then look at this — I am running again — yes —
I don't know why — no — but this is me racing —
sprinting — you could describe this motion as — *progress*,
I am sure, is too strong a word — you could describe this
motion as *variation* — *a change of state* — yes, surely that —
that, if nothing else — flying forward for minutes on end
— if we can call these losses minutes — call this forward
— if we can imagine time as a necklace — say minutes
and not decades — and next — my dash is done with me
— I am chuffing here — standing still in brainbusyness
— intervaling — you could describe this immobility as
intervaling — yes, surely that — that, if nothing else —
standing with my father beneath a lone olive tree one
morning cobwebby with pearled light, and — no — not
that — that was something else — that was some other
disappointment in the head.

::::: **DEBRIS**

Which is to say I have bled since birth. Maybe I should mention this. I was born bleeding. I will die bleeding.

Debris is the bleeding kind.

Meaning sometimes the problem is remembering too much and having no place to leave it all except in my mouth.

lance olsen

:::: **DEBRIS**

Mind, angel, Mommy whispering, suddenly with me, rocking Her Little Duration in her lap: *You don't need to learn to adapt to Daedalus' imagination. Survival is never mandatory.*

:::: **DEBRIS**

Not my father that morning cobwebby with pearled light, but Daedalus. Not me, but his twiggish apprentice Perdix. Not standing, but strolling. Not beneath an olive tree, but along the Athenian seashore.

When did stories become so difficult to tell?

Look: Perdix noticing a fish spine poking from pebbles, bending down to pick it up.

Back at the shop that afternoon, he imitates the spine's form by notching one edge of an iron slab and with that the saw enters the cosmos.

It didn't exist. It did.

Like a slap.

:::: **DEBRIS**

And rocking I repeat to Mommy what the screamings say to me, but I don't think she believes me.

She smiles and pats me on the head as if smiles were nothing except smiles.

Smiles, pats, closes her eyes, listening to something I can't make out.

Italics, maybe.

Ellipses.

:::: **DEBRIS**

I tell her the screamings tell me I will never have heard enough.

There will always be more.

They will always feel like waiting for something.

They tell me they will just keep arriving, keep rushing in.

This is how it will always be.

Until this is not how it will always be, evidently.

They tell me —

:::: **J. G. BALLARD SONG**

Because all clocks are labyrinths.

:::: **DEBRIS**

There. They have been silent for — who can say how long? — who can say what *long* means? — nearly silent — practically inaudible — except not exactly — there is a continuous rustle of murmurings — sounds like fluttery lights — and in any case I'm not convinced you could call what complicates the middle of my face a nose.

You could more accurately describe it as two purple-crimson slits winging up from the middle of a wide mouth jaggy with teeth.

Those moments the screamings withdraw like tiny shreds of death.

:::: **DEBRIS**

When did stories become frantic night sky, each jittering white speck precisely a jittering white speck and nothing else?

:::: **DEBRIS**

The sparse hair tufts patching my body are so pale you could mistake them for thoughts growing from my scalp, thighs, breast nubs.

Another way of saying this: the saw didn't exist, and then it did, like a slap, because Daedalus fears his apprentice's fame will someday surpass his own, and so early next morning he baits the boy to the megaron overlooking Athens for prayers.

I watch them standing alone, side by side, atop the outcrop, mentor and novice admiring the sun goldenly revolutionizing the whitewashed structures below.

Watch Daedalus reach out and clap Perdix between the shoulder blades affectionately, then not.

Watch the startled boy go over.

:::: **DEBRIS**

By that I mean imagine how death doesn't concern you. As long as you live, death is not with you, and when it is you are not alive.

Now imagine you are wrong.

:::: JORGE LUIS BORGES SONG

Because — *another* — *here comes another* — because time is a river which sweeps me along, yet I am the river; it is a tiger which destroys me, yet I am the tiger; it is a fire which consumes me, yet I am the fire.

:::: DEBRIS

It sometimes crosses my mind that I might frighten people.

People certainly frighten me.

Yet I think mostly they frighten themselves, being what they are.

:::: **DEBRIS**

The lump rising from my left shoulder is crammed with other people's recollections: a point perhaps worth mentioning.

Which is to say, by closing my eyes I can sometimes make out how, long ago, in the stinging white north, a degradation of fishermen walked to the center of a stone maze called the Giant's Garden, enticing all the evil spirits in the area to follow them, then dashed out to their boats and put to sea before those demons could bungle their way back into the open.

Later that day a blizzard hurled in and drowned every one of those fishermen.

:::: DEBRIS

For we all create stories to protect ourselves, Button, Mommy whispers, rocking.

[[Maybe she said this back in the age when hope still mattered.]]

Yet search as I might over the eons — if we may call them that — that and not something else — *miscalculations,* for instance — *vestigial unkindnesses* — I am running again — look at this — will wonders never cease? — never begin? — yet search as I might over the — whatever the word in the end might prove to be — I have never been able to locate the guarded portal of my own home — but surely it exists — somewhere among my heart's rummage — yes — in the same way, say, that future dictionaries exist — although — *listen* —

:::: **SIR ARTHUR EVANS SONG**

It was March 1900, the enamel sky a singular dry blue, the
air cool, invigorating, and —

:::: DEBRIS

— a delay — and they are back again — this seems to be my point — one by one by — this is how it has always been — how it always will be — until, obviously —

:::: SIR ARTHUR EVANS SONG

— and, both having secured the crucial wind-buffeted land, by means of generous private donations from the Cretan Exploration Fund made possible by my position as director of Oxford's Ashmolean, and having ordered stores from Britain, I hired two foremen from the most capable of the generally incapable (if ever childishly cheerful and rigorously uncurious) locals, who in turn hired two and thirty diggers, and —

:::: **DEBRIS**

Because misremembering, I sometimes find myself remembering, is an act —

:::: **SIR ARTHUR EVANS SONG**

— and the lot of them went merrily to work on the flower-covered hill beneath which I was certain lay the inconceivable ruins.

:::: **DEBRIS**

And one day — *keep it going* — *keep it going* —

:::: **DEBRIS**

And one day Mommy brought around Lady Tiresias.

Calling my name, listening for my response, calling again, she zeroed in on her little princess. Soon we were sitting cross-legged in a chamber I had never seen before.

It stank language.

Vowels, mostly.

The bony blind seer with wrinkled female dugs had known life as both man and woman. He enjoyed my pity. She reached for my hand. He wanted to read my palm. I hissed at her. He drew back. Mommy stroked my scruff.

Be nice, Button, she said, me growling under my wheeze, because misremembering is an act of the soul speaking with itself.

:::: **DEBRIS**

[[Because rock is always simply slow water.]]

:::: **DEBRIS**

Because one of the greatest pleasures down here — down where? — why should I be able to speak about thereness when unable to speak about whenness? — one of the greatest pleasures down here — yes — whatever such expressions might in the end convey — is the gorgeous sensation arising from petting myself against corners.

There are no words.

:::: DEBRIS

By that I mean Lady Tiresias discovered my palm bloated smooth as a baboon's ass: no bumps, lumps, fissures, figures, futures.

You are born, she said, of a very special race. The Minotaur belongs to a people old as the earth itself. Few know beneath the skin of your shoulders grow wings. Someday they will break free and carry you away from here.

I reached back and felt nothing.

Give yourself time, she said.

He said: The number thirty-three controls your life.

They — grammar by nature a category of error — they said: You are concerned not with personal ambition but with uplifting the loving energy of humankind.

:::: **DEBRIS**

Lady Tiresias' bald head reminded me of an enormous gland.

:::: **DEBRIS**

That afternoon Mommy led herhim to the Brazen Bull. The hollow bronze beast hulked on a raised platform in our central courtyard at the edge of the shallow pool swarming with eels, each sporting its own pair of bitsy gilt earrings.

Two Athenian slaves helped himher through the hatch in its side. Somewhere beyond the wall, greensilver olive leaves swished in the breeze across our whaled hills. The seer who could not see ordered the slaves to be careful. The slaves obeyed. I watched them shut and lock the hatch, watched them light the fire, listened to it crackle awake. Incense billowed from the Brazen Bull's nostrils.

A complex system of tubes and stops inside its skull translated the soothsayer's surprised shrieks into infuriated bovine bellows.

lance olsen

:::: **DEBRIS**

First comes pain, Mommy whispered, *then comes knowledge.*

:::: **HERAKLION ARCHEOLOGICAL MUSEUM SONG**

These red clay Linear A tablets recording quantities of cereal and personnel (rations?) survived the destruction horizon.

:::: **DEBRIS**

They come. They go. We know the voices as distances. When somebody touches us, this is what we feel.

Or I could tell you a different story. There are so many to choose from. Some are sad. Some are sadder. The end of each is dead air. I could tell you the one about how the following afternoon they opened the hatch and extracted what was left of our prophet. Mommy asked the most delicate bits be fashioned into my beautiful new bracelet.

I could show you with that story — let us call it a romance — how much Mommy loves Her Little Duration.

:::: **DEBRIS**

Or I could explain to you how before and after that I watched many wars. Or maybe I watched the same war many times. Explain to you how I watched the slow wreckage of my city bogging into the earth. Daedalus' boy attempting to scrabble up a hidden ladder above a seascape sheened like hammered silver, wax wings reducing to air around him. My sister Ariadne, whom I have never met, who has never called on me, not once, not ever, handing something I could not make out to a muscular young man I could not recognize standing in front of a gate I could not place.

:::: DEBRIS

Watched Daddy, whom I have never met, who has never called on me, not once, not ever, wearing only his gold necklace shaped like a string of lilies, reclining in a stone tub decorated with octopi and anemones, as the daughter of Cocalus, King of Camicus, signaled her slave to empty a pot not of warm water but of boiling oil over his head and chest and groin.

How the dying of his skin sounded like a field shrouded in locusts.

:::: **DEBRIS**

Or how there are stories that make sense. These are called lies. And how there are stories that maze you. These are called the whirled.

:::: **DEBRIS**

How your body is a haunted house from which you can never escape.

Except once.

:::: **LADY TIRESIAS CHORUS**

For when I die, it will have been inside the stomach of a bronze bull. It will have been inside the courtyard of a doomed palace. With the understanding that the descent into Hades is the same from every direction. That I shall soon meet Odysseus in a boundless cindery desert and, skin ashen, eyes cloudy and blank from too much seeing, violet mouth sewn shut with black catgut, he will ask me without using words to recollect what the best path of life is. And I shall advise the sacker of cities to forget the philosophers and their metaphysics. In the end there is nothing except atoms and empty space. That is it, that is all, that is us, that is this. I shall make clear to him no one will arrive to save us from ourselves. When I die, it will have been wondering whether I am actually thinking these thoughts or only dreaming I am thinking them as I study the glowing blue flame floating out of my chest.

:::: DEBRIS

Or I could tell you the one about Debris hanging weightless in her mommy's womb, strangling her almost-brother with his own umbilical cord, preparing to bestow upon her parents her first gift, which they would in turn mummify and boon back to her, a mutual sign of their abiding affection and respect.

:::: **DEBRIS**

[[And now? Does anyone see me now?]]

:::: **DEBRIS**

Unless, obviously, I am untruthing.

There is always that.

Or believe I am reporting facts when I am reporting something else.

Or believe I am reporting something else when I am accidentally reporting facts.

Or bel — *listen*:

:::: SOPHOCLES SONG

And Phaedrus shares this fable about the poet Simonides. The ship he is on is sinking, the other passengers madly scrambling to save their possessions. But the poet does not scramble. The poet stands idly by, taking in the mayhem around him. When the captain asks why he is not gathering his belongings, Simonides responds: *Everything that is me is already with me.*

:::: **DEBRIS**

Because rocking, Mommy whispers: *The average lifespan for a bull is twenty-eight years, honey.*

Her sounds star smearage.

:::: ODYSSEUS SONG

Because I have nothing more to say. Look at me. I am a poor old stranger here. My home is far away. Look at me. There is no one known to me in countryside or city. Look at me. I have become a warning there is no one who can prevent necessity from happening.

:::: **DEBRIS**

Or I could tell you the one about Daedalus' trial and banishment by the Athenian courts for murdering Perdix.

How a swineherd found the artificer washed upon our shores and led him to the palace. Impressed by his talent, Daddy took him in, designated him royal architect. Not long after, Mommy fell in lust with a giant white bull sent by Poseidon to penalize her for being herself. She ordered Daedalus to build her a wooden cow draped in hide to fool the bull into squalling her.

Whenever you listen to Debris, you are really listening to the echo of Mommy and that bull coupling through the night in a damp rocky field at the edge of Knossos.

:::: **DEBRIS**

In their chronicles the historians refer to that echo as The Daedalus Penance.

[[They refer to it as The Wind Calamity.]]

:::: **DEBRIS**

And there was a day Mommy brought around Apis the Healer.

I was very young. I could barely toddle across a chamber from wall to wall. Apis carried a clay bowl stacked with pastry squares made from paper-thin sheets of dough layered with chopped dates, honey, and a buttery oil mixed with Athenian blood. Grinning, he passed me one. I gobbled it up and barked for another. He obliged. Then he eased me out of Mommy's arms, where I'd been rocking, and set me on the floor. He pressed his palm against my chest until I was lying flat on my back, chewing.

I recall the ceiling was especially high that day. Catastrophe propped in a corner, observing this unfolding with routine indifference.

lance olsen

:::: **PASIPHAË CHORUS**

— and when the midwife pulled the steaming godshit
from between my legs I took one look and commanded
kill it kill it kill the inaccuracy but my husband chuckled above
me saying *this bounty is yours sunshine a reward from the noises
for how you've lived your life* and with that he ordered the wet
nurse to deliver his wife's living failure into the labyrinth's
flections deep beneath their bed and —

:::: DEBRIS

By that I mean I don't understand time. For me it occurs as a commotion dazzle. By that I mean it is time only in its not being itself. I understand its essence perfectly until I try to explain to myself what it isn't.

And yet I am certain my battle with Apis has never ended.

I am certain it is still going on within this instant.

:::: **PASIPHAË CHORUS**

— and Minos strode out of the birthing chamber and out of my love and before that day drowned itself in the wine-dark sea my godshit had been tucked away from our citizens' eyes and ears forever and I had discovered just how much a woman can hate a man how much you think this affliction is all the loathing you can fist inside yourself only to learn there can always be more and after that more still because —

:::: **DEBRIS**

And then Apis began to probe me. He pried back my eyelids. Prodded my abdomen. Forced open my mouth to inspect my teeth.

I tried to convince myself he was petting me and leaned into his hand.

But an oily finger slipped between my thighs and Debris winced and snapped and all at once seconds began flocking into her head.

:::: LEONARDO DA VINCI SONG

In other words, even though both maze and labyrinth seem to depict a complex and confusing series of routes, no two designs could be more disparate; the maze being a complex branching conundrum that includes choices of path and direction, even as the labyrinth is unicursal, by which is meant a single, non-branching way leading to a center we might designate as heavenly affirmation. For the labyrinth possesses but one entrance, and that entrance also be its exit; while the diabolical maze possesses many points of ingress and egress.

:::: DEBRIS

Chortling somewhere above me, Apis said — he said: *A little fighter, isn't she?* — pinning me down more firmly.

lance olsen

:::: THE TERRIBLE ANGELS SONG

Stupid. So stupid. You and you and —

:::: **PROFESSOR VEIT ERLMANN SONG**

— and we may recall it was Apis the Healer, personal physician to the Roman emperor Marcus Aurelius, who first compared the inner ear to a labyrinth. A philosopher as well as one of the most accomplished medical researchers of antiquity, Apis was no doubt aware of the myth of Theseus and the Minotaur. The inward spiraling structure he found in dogs and monkeys — Roman law prohibited dissection of humans — surely suggested to him the sense of danger, loss, and even fear such forms are said to have evoked.

lance olsen

:::: **DEBRIS**

Listen: my lungs little gales.

:::: **ABDULLAH IBN UMAR SONG**

[[Because you must move through this world as if you were a stranger or a traveler.]]

:::: **THE TERRIBLE ANGELS SONG**

Jump. Jump now. Do it. Just to see what happens.

:::: **DEBRIS**

Mommy lowering herself to help Apis hold down my legs.

lance olsen

:::: **PROFESSOR ANNE P. CHAPIN SONG**

Therefore most early and mid-twentieth-century scholars understood Aegean landscape painting primarily in secular terms — as room decoration that rejoiced in the beauty of the natural world. Late twentieth-century scholars, however, have reconstructed a religious function for some, if not all. This later generation has recognized the importance of variability and uncertainty in their research: many frescoes, for instance, have been over-restored or restored incorrectly; the functions of the buildings in which frescoes were found are imperfectly under —

:::: **DEBRIS**

Mommy lowering herself to help Apis hold down my legs
and all at once a rapture of flies overrunning my face.
Because all at once there was that room and there was
another. Because outside that other room lay a corridor.
Because a rapture of flies overran my face and then I was
in that corridor outside that other room, closing in from
behind on one of my donations.

:::: **SAINT AUGUSTINE SONG**

— and both labyrinth and maze bring to mind the symbolic journey from this riven world to the next; both embody three-dimensional maps we walk not only on but through, confounding the difference between design and creation. Traversing either, the wanderer identifies with the course he follows even as he identifies with the overall composition of that course — this being the same relationship as a single word to an entire paragraph, a single page to an entire book, a single soul to God's mind.

:::: **DEBRIS**

She was taller than most and her hair long and abundant and black as deep space. She wore a white sacrificial tunic over which draped a purple shawl adorned with detailed geometric designs. Somehow she heard my feet chafing as I made my final advance. Sensing the density of my companionship, she turned and dropped to her knees to beg for her life.

:::: **PROFESSOR ANNE P. CHAPIN SONG**

Perhaps the most famous error of this sort remains Arthur Evans' misreading and consequent flawed restoration of the Saffron Gatherer fresco. Fragments of the original were excavated in 1900 in the area of the Early Keep. Evans guided the Swiss artist Émile Gilliéron on the undertaking. (Interesting to note, by the way, that Gilliéron's most distinguished pupil was Giorgio de Chirico, whose later paintings, such as *Ariadne*, drew heavily both on the mythology and architecture of Knossos.) Although Evans interpreted the fragments as parts of the body of a boy stooping among a field of crocuses, truth is blue monkeys abound in Aegean wall paintings; part of this one's tail, unrecognized at the time of restoration, is clearly visible at the far right. The boy had been a blue monkey all along. All one had to do to see was learn to look.

:::: **DEBRIS**

[[Maybe I should mention sometimes I don't understand the language I am using.]]

:::: **DEBRIS**

[[Maybe I should mention sometimes I do.]]

:::: **DEBRIS**

She turned and dropped to her knees to beg for her life, except Mommy's Little Duration had other ideas. She scurried full speed for the maiden's flawless nose and red lips in a teeth-hectic kiss.

Her last garbled word, I want to say, was a portion of my name.

:::: DAEDALUS SONG

9. Glass Breaths. Flying machines rendered invisible by mirror-skins reflecting sky, clouds, a percussion of giants.

:::: **DEBRIS**

Apis concluded I was nothing if not bright, barren, and already remarkably strong. Yet how long I would live, he told Mommy, he couldn't guess. Havocs like me often survived less than a breath, occasionally an hour or a day or a month or a year, infrequently two or three. Yet never longer, for we enter the world with the express purpose, not of lingering, but of reminding others the best thing for humans to do is not to have been born in the first place and, if it is regrettably already too late, then to desist from that misunderstanding as quickly as possible.

:::: **DEBRIS**

By that I mean the historians chronicle how my daddy showed King Aegeus the purity of his ideas for fewer than two sunrises before the soldiers lining his ramparts agreed with him and lifted their shields above their heads in capitulation. As an afterthought, Daddy flayed every tenth one and nailed the skin flags along the city wall.

This gesture was meant to express to the Athenian ruler Daddy's deep appreciation for the war King Aegeus had poked awake around him.

:::: **DAEDALUS SONG**

2. Religion, or Vessel of Accidental Speech. An automata army whose complex systems of pulleys and gears driven by miniature steam engines are sheltered in suits of black armor covered with poison spikes: a battalion of human sea urchins spilling at you across the scrubby landscape.

:::: **DEBRIS**

Wolfing what remained of those pastries, I heard Apis spell out how he would, if it suited the queen, examine his patient on a regular basis. I heard Mommy not disagreeing. I heard him hesitate, then add he would consider it the greatest honor if, when the umber inevitable arrived, he were to be granted permission to dissect Her Majesty's Little Duration. I heard Mommy not disagreeing again.

What I am telling you, I want to say, is a story about how deeply family members can care for one another.

:::: **DEBRIS**

What I am telling you is there is blue enamel sky and wind-churned waves that look like white dolphins leaping.

But not here.

:::: DAEDALUS SONG

7. Water Teeth. Submarines mounted with gigantic blades designed to splinter enemy ships in harbor before they can begin to consider raising anchor to flee.

10. Behavior Apostle. A fleet of scythed chariots designed to cause enemy soldiers to forget their wives and children.

3. Rape Garden. A pitying of —

:::: **DEBRIS**

The historians chronicle how, when my brother Androgeos, whom I have never met, not once, not ever, started to collect all the prizes at the Panathenaic games, King Aegeus commanded him to fight his most fearsome bull in the bull-leaping competition, and how Androgeos agreed.

Forty seconds later my brother lay bewildered and gored on the sandy stadium floor.

:::: SAINT THOMAS AQUINAS SONG

Strictly speaking, I mean to inquire: is the labyrinth a plan for a prison, or the instructions for a dance?

:::: DEBRIS

Androgeos bleeding out beneath the shameful lemon sky.

:::: THE TERRIBLE ANGELS SONG

Stupid. You're so stupid. Look at you. Look at what you've done now. Jump. JUMP.

:::: DEBRIS

Because, outraged by my brother's murder, Daddy set off to Athens, revenge searing in his veins. Along the way he invaded Megara, whose King Nisos' power derived from a single lock of purple hair. Nisos' daughter Scylla saw Daddy from the battlements, tumbled into love with him in the beat of a hurt, and that night sheared her father as if he were a feebleminded sheep pinned in a catching pen.

:::: **DEBRIS**

Because, strictly speaking, Debris understands there are no more innocent people in the world, although this morning — let us call it morning — I find myself roaming — roaming and howling — howling a —

:::: DAEDALUS SONG

3. Rape Garden. A pitying of huge crossbows — each the length of a dozen men lying helmet to boot — boasting worm-and-gear mechanisms to draw the bowstrings; wooden barrel projectiles swelled with incense to induce adversaries to discover curiosity in their surroundings, thereby turning their backs on the battle before them.

:::: DEBRIS

— howling and dragging my nails along the walls as I advance — *advance* perhaps evoking too strong an act — and it may be evening instead — let us call it that — call it evening — midday — I find myself roaming and howling and dragging my nails along the walls in a particularly damp branch of passageways — inventing them as I go — passageways I have never stumbled upon before — even though it may be the case I have stumbled upon similar ones — or for all I know I *have* stumbled upon these before — only to have forgotten them — as I have forgotten so many things in my life — lives — which — because I have forgotten them — I am almost surely unaware of having forgotten — remembering only the act of grayish disremembering.

:::: **DEBRIS**

Appalled before Scylla's lack of filial devotion, Daddy departed at once, leaving her keening on the dock.

Each star in the night sky a pinprick upon her skin.

:::: **DEBRIS**

By that I mean *networks*. *Weaves*. How each of us becomes hole.

:::: **DEBRIS**

Because Scylla didn't give up, but dived into the sea to swim after Daddy's ship, and some say it is even conceivable she might have reached it, had Nisos not —

lance olsen

:::: **DEBRIS**

Wait. I believe I've just had a dream.

:::: **DEBRIS**

— had Nisos not blurred himself into an osprey and swooped down to destroy her.

lance olsen

:::: **DEBRIS**

Yes: there's no other noun for it.

:::: **DEBRIS**

Because at the last instant Nisos' daughter quivered into
a tiny storm petrel that darted away from her father over
the white dolphining waves.

:::: **DEBRIS**

Yet Scylla's father pursued.

:::: **DEBRIS**

Because Scylla's daddy wouldn't forget.

:::: **DEBRIS**

Although it is equally possible I've just had a vision instead. Or a memory of the future. Yes — we could say: *I believe I have just had a thought from tomorrow.*

:::: **DEBRIS**

Because now and forever Nisos is one beak clip away from tattering Scylla into a burst of bloody feathers.

:::: **DEBRIS**

[[Or perhaps a memory from tomorrow just had me.]]

:::: **DEBRIS**

And in this dream — this dream or memory — if we should choose to name this agitation such a thing — the muscular young man I couldn't recognize to whom my sister Ariadne had handed something I couldn't make out stood before the alabaster throne in a palace so sun-flooded the lavish furniture itself seemed assembled out of shimmering silver haze.

He was addressing someone. I couldn't make out whom. I couldn't make out what he was saying or what land he was saying it in.

Still, all at once his lips parted — I dreamed — and I heard him speak my name — one of my names — *look at you — you and you and you* — and I balked awake into a rush of Mommy whispers — *once upon a beast — once upon a beast —*

:::: PASIPHAË CHORUS

And there was a day, she was saying, *a beast called the Bull of Heaven crashed into being.*

Its very amplitude lowered the level of rivers, opened vast pits that swallowed hundreds of men, women, and children.

After many years of destruction, a courageous young warrior from a far-off shore appeared to slay the monster. A horrendous battle ensued. Villages became gaps in syntax. Topography became hypothetical. Time turned the color of ice and melted.

Standing over the behemoth's corpse, the foreigner offered up its still-beating heart to the noises. In the heart of that heart lived a little girl's voice. It was singing.

The noises accepted the foreigner's gift.

By way of thanks they translated our world into a whorl of craving and aporia.

:::: DEBRIS

Unless I am still asleep, or — *listen*:

:::: STUXNET SONG

We are Stuxnet, the first computer worm designed specifically to cause material damage by forcing a large number of —

:::: DEBRIS

How can these voices that aren't mine always have been mine?

:::: STUXNET SONG

— by forcing a large number of Iran's centrifuges used to enrich uranium to spin out of control and —

:::: DEBRIS

— and what I am doing now, doing then, doing next, doing once, doing last, doing forever, is this: I am squatting at the juncture of two corridors. Moisture slips down the walls. Mildew entertains the air. Every time a plump rat waddles around the corner in search of water, I pounce.

The crackle of snapping necks.

The popping of brittle skulls.

Debris chewing, sucking, squatting, listening, cheerful, life juices dribbling down her shiny chin, because —

:::: PROFESSOR ROBERT HERMAN SONG

Because traffic streams behave like fluids.

:::: BENOIT MANDELBROT SONG

Because a cloud is made of billows upon billows of other clouds. Come closer, and you don't get something smooth, but irregularities at a smaller scale that —

:::: STUXNET SONG

— spin out of control and self-destruct. We initially spread indiscriminately via Microsoft Windows, but included in us was a highly specialized payload designed to target only Siemens supervisory control and data acquisition systems. Uncovered in 2010, we first contaminated the Natanz facility, 210 miles south of Tehran, one year earlier.

:::: **DEBRIS**

Or perhaps one could say this is the dream and the other thing the other thing, or there will always be facts I regret knowing, and, having eaten my fill, I leave behind a few rat carcasses sans heads for Daedalus and Icarus to find as they roam just before me, behind, beside, below, above, rummaging for the exit to my sacred knot.

:::: PROFESSOR ROBERT HERMAN SONG

Because traffic streams behave like fluids. Waves ripple through them as cars adjust their speed. Gridlock emerges when a single driver rides his brakes a split second too long. Yet, although motorists may be analogous to water particles, there is one profound difference complicating to an almost unimaginable degree the application of chaos theory to traffic patterns: motorists are particles with purpose.

:::: DEBRIS

Meaning in my dreams — I hear above me the palace's daily commotion — carts' wooden wheels clacking over uneven stones — peacock cries — men and women chattering — hammers slamming down on anvils — water trickling through drainage gutters as though a rain that will never stop — because the mask called my face — this is the point — I use the term loosely — because the mask called my face sometimes becomes a thousand honeybees made of black light and — and above the avocado greens — the mints and mosses — the rusted oranges — white-winged terns stall against a heavy breeze.

:::: BRADLEY MANNING SONG

Because it was not until I was in Iraq and reading secret military reports on a daily basis that I started to question the morality of what we were doing. This is why I turned over the files to which I had access to WikiLeaks, which made them public. I understand my actions violated the law. I regret that my actions hurt anyone or harmed the United States.

It was never my intent to hurt anyone. I only wanted to help people and —

:::: **PASIPHAË CHORUS**

— and I bore the bastard Acacallis bore him Ariadne bore him Androgeos bore him Catreus bore him Deucalion bore him Glaucus bore him Phaedra bore him Xenodice yet still my husband makes a daily art of amnesia refusing to mention the mistake barking up at us into our sleep every night refusing to think about —

dreamlives of debris

:::: ATHENA CHORUS

:::: **PASIPHAË CHORUS**

— about the boundless perplexity webbing below our feet and every day I have a greater sense that how to say it that I have begun to approximate myself yes a greater sense that I am gradually becoming the imprecision of Pasiphaë a cousin say or perhaps friend yes a friend who stopped writing the queen decades ago and —

:::: DEBRIS

— and how, when the breeze enlivened at sunset, the soldiers' hides shivered in a long diaphanous chain down the Megarian city wall.

Keepsakes, Daddy called them.

Welcome home poems.

:::: DEBRIS

And so, whispers Mommy out of the darkness, rocking, *consider all the beauty still left around you and be joyful.*

:::: THE TERRIBLE ANGELS SONG

Is that you? That's not you. It can't be you because you're nothing.

:::: DEBRIS

Because, as we all know, Minotaurs have nothing to do with the perpetuation of life.

The very idea of multiplication disgusts us.

:::: ANDRES SEVTSUK SONG

And conurbations exhibit a physical infrastructure that can be abstractly represented and reduced to three basic elements: links, or paths along which travel occurs; nodes, or the intersections where two or more paths cross and hence public spaces form; and buildings, where the movement of goods, people, and information begins or ends. Such a framework allows us to see how —

:::: **TOHONO O'ODHAM TRIBAL MEMBER SONG**

… how I was told … Elder Brother lived in the maze …
and the reason why he lived in the maze was because … I
think how I'm gonna say this … magician or, oh, medicine
man that can disappear … and that can do things … heal
people and things like that … that was Elder Brother …
Se:he, they called him …

:::: ROBERT & JEAN HOLLANDER SONG

Dante, whom the heretic Farinata degli Uberti warned may not see his home again (10.22-51), meets the Minotaur as Virgil leads him down the boulder-strewn path toward the first ring of the seventh circle (12.11-24). To Virgil and Dante's left flows a river of boiling blood from which cry out sinners who have performed violence against their neighbors. The boulders, Virgil explains, are the result of the earthquake triggered by Christ's harrowing of Hell. All at once the Minotaur, guardian of this circle of violence, steps from behind a cluster of those boulders into the —

:::: **THE TERRIBLE ANGELS SONG**

Go ahead, you pitiful fuck. At twenty-three percent you never know what might —

:::: **DEBRIS**

Or I could tell you about how before and after that I watched Paris steal Helen — herself a maze within a maze — from her husband. Watched black flames lick through a decade. Watched beautiful broken Cassandra — pale skin, blue eyes, red hair kept in curls, raped repeatedly by Ajax the Lesser on the floor of Athena's temple where she had fled in search of refuge — beautiful broken Cassandra babble from the post to which she had been tied before the gates of junked Troy — disinterested pedestrians passing her by as if she were an unhinged beggar — as if she were the —

:::: **ROBERT & JEAN HOLLANDER SONG**

— the Minotaur all at once steps from behind a cluster of those boulders into the open, and, at the sight of Dante and Virgil, it commences gnawing at its own shoulder: even, we are told, as one whom anger racks within. When Virgil mentions the Minotaur's executioner to his ward, the creature bucks frenetically, because —

:::: **DEBRIS**

— because I seem to be speaking. I understand how you could arrive at such a faulty conclusion. But these word turbulences aren't mine. Do not seem to be mine. Do and do not seem to be mine. What I mean to say is, I am nearly convinced my mouth is vigorously not moving.

:::: I LOVE YOU SONG

Because millions of people one day innocently opened our email attachment labeled *I love you*. That click unleashed a virus whose objective was to overwrite those people's image files, then email itself to the first fifty contacts in their address books. Within six hours our malware had become a global pandemic.

::: **TOHONO O'ODHAM TRIBAL MEMBER SONG**

… Se:he … yes… Elder Brother … that's how they tell it … but he had a lot of enemies so he made that … his maze … to live in there … and people would go in there but they couldn't find him … so they would turn around and go back out …

:::: DEBRIS

And Daedalus' crimped gray face carries the same message wherever it goes: *I have come to understand the best one can hope for is to have a relationship with the blank where God would be if there were no blank.* And before and after that I watched a beautiful broken teen whose name I couldn't make out dangling from a mango tree in a damp rocky field near the Indian village of Katra Sadatganj, where she had been roped and raped repeatedly, disinterested pedestrians passing her by as if —

:::: **DEBRIS**

And then one morning — this morning — let us call it this morning — and not another — nor evening — midday — let us say this morning I entered a chamber to rest.

Rising to move on, I discovered I could no longer locate the doorway. I assumed at first I was groping the wrong wall. I made a slow survey with my free hand, Catastrophe rooting me on, but encountered nothing except gritty blank surfaces, low voices murmuring in the walls, and parentheses.

What, I wondered, if this were another Daedalus trick? If the door were gone for good? Debris could starve in here. Debris could become unremembered.

I panicked and the walls around me exploded into —

:::: I LOVE YOU SONG

What we are telling you is one evening a muscular black teen in Kinshasa innocently slipped a forkful of infected chimpanzee meat between his lips.

It unleashed a strain of simian immunodeficiency virus into his system. The virus overwrote the teen's DNA files, slowly mutating as it did so into the human immunodeficiency virus, a biological malware causing acquired immunodeficiency syndrome, a condition in which progressive failure of the immune system allows opportunistic infections and cancers to blossom.

Because there is metaphor and there is metaphor.

What we are telling you is within sixty years AIDS had become a global pandemic.

:::: **DEBRIS**

The walls around me exploded into shocked Icarus dropping through luminous blueness — hands raking sunlight — shredded wings coming apart in mid-flight — a miniature cloud of gray-white commas — and I watched as Daddy locked Daedalus and son deep inside my nightnothing — watched them stumbling forward — scouring my heart for an outlet.

:::: **DEBRIS**

The walls around me exploded into a whirl of knife blades. The whirl of knife blades exploded into an applause of white hands. The applause of white hands exploded into a mischief of mice. The mischief of mice exploded into a zeal of invisible tigers. The zeal of invisible tigers exploded into an ambush of orange shrieks. And I came to understand in that instant everything was as it should be, had always been, would always be, more or less, roughly speaking, give or take.

And so I crouched to wait out the hot blood drizzle that had begun falling around me.

:::: **PLINY THE ELDER SONG**

Nonetheless, we must not, comparing this particular labyrinth to what we see delineated on our mosaic pavements, or to the mazes formed in fields for the amusement of children, suppose it to be a narrow promenade along which we may walk for many miles together; but rather picture to ourselves a building filled with numerous doors and galleries which incessantly mislead the visitor, bringing him back, after all his wanderings, to the spot from which he first set out, causing him to wonder —

:::: DEBRIS

[[Am I perhaps being heard?]]

:::: TOHONO O'ODHAM TRIBAL MEMBER SONG

... you fall and you feel bad ... only you pick yourself up and you go on through the maze ... so many places in there you might ... you get up, turn around, go again ... and when you reach that middle of the maze ... that's when you see the Sun God and the Sun God blesses you in a dream and says you have made it ... and that's where you die ...

:::: **DEBRIS**

And then one morning — this morning — let us call it this morning — and not another — yesterday — tomorrow — let us call it the fragrance of copper ingots from Cyprus made moist in your palm — and then one morning there appears blue enamel sky hovering sun-rushed above the dream stranger sitting cross-legged, alone, on the same pebbly beach where Perdix, strolling beside Daedalus, once bent down (will bend down, is bending down) to pick up his mortality. A thrill passes through the dream stranger's chest as he sharpens a bronze dagger against a whetstone cradled in his lap. He hums without knowing he is humming, thinks without knowing he is thinking. *I will do this thing*, the idea flitters across his mind in bright splinters, *and then I will do this thing, and then I will do the other, and then it will be done.*

:::: **DEBRIS**

A thrill passes through the dream stranger's chest as he sharpens a bronze dagger against a whetstone cradled in his lap. He hums without knowing he is humming, thinks without knowing he is thinking.

I will do this thing, the idea flitters across his mind in bright splinters, *and then I will do this thing, and then I will do the other, and then it will be done.*

:::: **DEBRIS**

Hell to ships, hell to men, hell to cities — and Clytemnestra clawing a dagger across Cassandra's bared throat — Agamemnon returned to Mycenae with the disbelieved seer his war spoil — Clytemnestra's rage — and before and after that I watched an arrow pierce swift-footed Achilles' heel — his body pitch forward into death's embrace — watched him — watched Achilles — no trace of his own ruin shadowing his features — slit the heels of Hector's corpse — pass Ajax's belt through the red gashes — drag the breaker of horses around and around the fortress walls — Hector's body erasing itself into the rocky earth — watched him — watched it — watched as —

:::: **ROBERT & JEAN HOLLANDER SONG**

Some commentators note it is unclear from the descriptions whether Dante portrays the Minotaur with the head of a bull and body of a man, vice versa, or in some other configuration entirely. Scholars have argued all three possibilities to different ends. Whatever the case, the hybrid beast for Dante represents the precise opposite of fourteenth-century Christian ideals. While elsewhere the Minotaur has been interpreted as the representation of Minos' private life, the Freudian unconscious, political power sans ethics, the tormenter and victim that live within each of us, infinite desire loosed (or imprisoned and repressed), the devouring maternal in whom both womb and grave exist simultaneously, and epitome of Derrida's monstrous thinking-otherwise, here the beast signifies the embodiment of man become blind brute, the quintessence of evil undoing itself, because —

:::: **DEBRIS**

Because what I am telling you is a story about how living at home is never an option.

:::: **DEBRIS**

Which is to say something is beginning.

[[Isn't it?]]

But here, but now, we haven't yet reached that point.

Meaning we arrived long ago.

Meaning when I hear people laugh, I imagine they are in Heaven.

:::: **SIR ARTHUR EVANS SONG**

Because we are Englishmen, and so were not accustomed
to being stymied by the mystifying local bureaucracies
we encountered over the course of our spadework on
Crete, this despite my inner understanding of the native
population, for whom I construed myself both comrade
and master.

:::: **DEBRIS**

Meaning the worst is still to come, was still to come, will still be to come, has come, had come, is coming, has been coming, might come, will have come, would have come, but not today, and already.

:::: **PLINY THE ELDER SONG**

Because only a single person has ever made repairs to the structure subdivided into numberless regions and prefectures; that being Chaeremon, eunuch of King Necthebis, who lived five hundred years before the time of Alexander the Great.

:::: DEBRIS

Or I could tell you about how one day it crossed my mind to scratch marks into the walls at each intersection to crumb my tracks.

Before long I began to see them reappear, patterning into advice. I rejoiced at the progress I was making — until it struck me they might not be my marks at all — could just as easily be Daedalus' — Icarus' — one of my visitors' — employed to crumb *their* tracks — or deliberately mislead me — yes — there was always that possibility among others — at which point I put an end to my experiment. *Because if this is paradise*, I decided, as some of our greatest philosophers have surmised, *I don't understand what it is for*.

Hard as I try, I have never been able to locate any of those marks again.

:::: **DEBRIS**

Or I could describe the sound of Lady Tiresias' bracelet clicking with herhis bits on my wrist as I prowl, Daedalus and his son always palming their way along just a few hundred paces in front of me, behind me, beside me, searching, choosing on a whim to believe the feeling they are experiencing must be happiness.

lance olsen

:::: **DEBRIS**

[[Another way of saying this: *How did it get so late so soon?*]]

:::: **CHAEREMON CHORUS**

; for my heart is a house of dust through which I shuffle, tidying, yet the undoing steadily outpaces me; I sweep this passageway, only to find it powdered over next day; I fasten back into place that fallen stone, only to find several others have come loose during the night; some fifty years ago I set for myself what I thought to be modest lifework: rebuild each chamber throughout the level upon which I originally stumbled; yet I have been unsuccessful at rebuilding even part of the first one of these; there aren't enough Chaeremons for the task; there is too much world; even so, I confess this to be a peaceful defeat;

:::: **CATASTROPHE CHORUS**

accuse me

It is

true

but it is also true

Shall I repeat

The sun

of a child

gathered stones.

nothing is communicable by   .

lance olsen

                                                            I let myself fall

until I am bloody.

                  But of all the games, I prefer the one about the
other   . I pretend that   comes
to visit me and

           The house is the same size as the world;

Perhaps I have created the stars

my redeemer

my redeemer

:::: **DEBRIS**

By that I mean I love my mommy, yet sometimes I love my daddy more.

Is this not the case with all children — one parent feeling a kindred spirit, the other a distant acquaintance? Debris is first to realize the king must be too busy to visit her. After all, he is a great ruler with many important schemes in need of his attention: a man of action, thoughtful calculations, a scholar.

Still, she knows he always keeps his daughter tucked away among his ideas like a pennyroyal seed between a pair of molars.

:::: **DEBRIS**

By that I mean the dream stranger dancing among thirteen sacrifices — seven beautiful women, six handsome men — to a rattling sistrum, three beats and pause, three beats and pause, beneath a pinpricked night sky before a temple's torchlit entrance.

:::: DANIELLE STEELE SONG

I mean, how can you fall asleep in this shitty hotel with a new character barking up at you into your dreams? She's right there, clear as day: Google exec in a boardroom, listening to her team laying out the latest strategies for organizing the world's data. Snow-white hair cut in a sleek bob. High cheekbones. Angular face. Fifteen-year-old daughter at home in Chicago exchanging bodily fluids with a flowchart of fellow tenth-graders. The exec's been sitting stone silent, taking in everything around her with those quick, sharp, intense enamel-blue eyes of hers. Her name is — is — All at once she's speaking, interrupting the presentation. She leans back in her chair, declaring in no uncertain terms — *what*? What does she declare in no uncertain terms? Oh, fuck it: I'll go on Twitter and see what everyone's saying about me.

:::: DEBRIS

Because before and after that I watched an elderly seamstress with a question-mark backbone — she was meticulously embroidering into one small corner of the Bayeux Tapestry's sprawl — meticulously embroidering into it the unassuming image of Halley's Comet — cartoon rocket above cartoon castle — Sun God screaming in her head — and — and the dream stranger rises — dagger in hand on that pebbly beach — rises and surveys the choppy sky-sea the color of a gull's dull wing — although he can't remember noticing it change — the sky — the sea — its complexion — one second enamel blue — the next this — yet it doesn't matter — he doesn't care — that previous moment is only an idea now — and with a quick pivot he cracks his back and steps into —

:::: **BRADLEY MANNING SONG**

— into the next phase of my life, I want everyone to know the real me. I am Chelsea Manning. I am a female. Given the way I feel, and have felt since childhood, I want to begin hormone therapy as soon as possible. I hope that you will support me in this passage.

I also request that, starting today, you refer to me by my new name and use the feminine pronoun.

:::: **CHAEREMON CHORUS**

; and so I shuffle through my ceaseless error, torch and broom in hand, small pack of food and wine strapped across my shoulders, wifeless, childless, dogless, loveless, meditating upon how, as I move, the minutes swell into an Alexandrian Library of decades; in the majority of manuscripts housed there I don't exist; you don't exist; nor does any knowledge of these passageways among which I have smoldered away my life; I chew on these sour facts, bad-kneeing along, content as much as one eunuch can be about not grasping where he is, or when, or why; biding his time until whichever noise is enjoying his predicament decides to cease his or her divine retribution for a trespass he can't recall ever having committed;

:::: **DEBRIS**

I love my daddy more, yet I watch him die many times
a day: at Camicus in scraggy Sicily, that fortress erected
by Daedalus amid stony outcroppings for King Cocalus
after the artificer fled my heart, disguised himself as an
old beggar, melted into Cocalus' vanity.

Because faith is an intrusion inside me.

Because watching is like trying to look at a minute.

:::: DETENTION SITE COBALT SONG

Negative, sir. The medical officer didn't seem, um, super worried about the, uh, you know, the gastric juices fucking with KSM's esophagus or anything. What? Khalid Shaikh Mohammad. Affirmative. He told us we were basically just doing a series of fake drownings. It wasn't like anything could happen or — What? It's weird. I mean, honestly, you just sort of, um, do it. You do this thing. Then you do the next thing. And pretty soon you're done, and — What? Uh, I don't get the question. Could you please rephrase?

:::: DEBRIS

— because before and after that I watched the dream
stranger kneeling before an altar inside the temple in
a brume of votive candles — he was snapping in half a
figurine representing himself — at the feet of a priest —
then carefully gluing it back together again — the priest
chanting above him — until — assisted by —

:::: **SIR ARTHUR EVANS SONG**

— assisted by my second in command, Dr. Duncan Mackenzie, one cheerfully pessimistic Scotsman in possession of an estimable doctorate from Vienna (a genuine professional, I should add, who had already distinguished himself through a series of fine excavations on Melos), and one Mr. Fyfe, an easily agitated yet quite accomplished and affable architect from the British School at Athens, we had within only a few months uncovered what I believed to be a substantial portion of the palace of Minos, an exceptional structure that revealed itself to be an intricate collection of over one thousand interlocking rooms, and —

:::: **DEBRIS**

And I watched hundreds of wide-winged cubes hang in a desert of silence 22,236 miles above the equator — watched them — watched me — watched as —

:::: **DEBRIS**

— as Apis the Healer started coming around more often. At first Mommy accompanied him, but soon he began shambling from the darkness alone, calling my name, torch in one hand, in the other his bowl of auras. Sometimes he examined me. Sometimes, his attention elsewhere, I secretly pet myself against his knuckles. Sometimes he carried with him a box of paints and small wooden board, wanting, he said, to render me for future physicians and philosophers. I watched as he hoisted me onto a raised slab. Watched as he posed me. Chin tilted up slightly, face slightly left.

Mixing pigments with egg yolk, Apis the Healer dabbed me into being, saying as he worked —

— saying —

:::: APIS THE HEALER SONG

If we could slow down the hot dusty winds that blow across Crete from the south, we would see inside them each dead father who ever lived sledgehammering to pieces his own dead father, and those dead fathers sledgehammering to pieces their own dead fathers, and so on back to the first dead father, who was the size of existence itself and boasted everything any father could boast except body and behavior.

:::: **DEBRIS**

Because my heart — this house of dust through which
I sometimes — I don't know why — through which I
sometimes break into an all-out bolt — dodging scattered
rat bones — sidestepping shattered stone lamps —
smashed pottery busy with spirals — double-headed axes
splintered down hallways — break into an all-out bolt —
until I can't go on anymore — collapse dizzy on the floor
— lack of Saturdays and prepositions wheeling around
me — and wait for the temporal rush to stop — almosting
— and then — slowly — rising — slowly hunkering down
— breaking into an all-out bolt anew.

:::: DEBRIS

By that I mean I love my daddy more, yet I watch him approach King Cocalus, that dull waddling fop in the long crimson cape and preposterous golden slippers, to ask the same riddle he has asked every leader on his long journey across the great sea: *How do you string a spiral seashell all the way through without damaging it?* And I reach into tomorrow shimmer to tell Daddy to stop it. Come home to his other fate. And he parts his lips without hearing me.

:::: DEBRIS

The dream stranger mans an oar in a black-prowed galley scudding beneath a fiery white sun — yes — that's it — I see him staring out over the ocean's endless waste — tumbling into a reverie about —

    — about what? —

    — about —

:::: DEBRIS

— about me skittering headlong through my murder of routes — hoofs and brother raised above my head — tears streaming down my face — feeling Mommy's Little Duration becoming somebody else's past — crying out: *Help me! Help me! Please, somebody, help me!* — but those cries issue with the intonations of cordial conversation — we could produce no better — and so you stopped them — *you and you and you* — I slowed their blundering dash — lowered our arms and her Catastrophe — continued on my way at a more leisurely panic — watching dogs in every city on every island in the world erupting into men — rising up on their hind legs to comment on the weather — their voices speaking from within these walls — saying —

:::: **THE TERRIBLE ANGELS SONG**

Facebook futures at twenty-three percent. Data mining. Rape pages. Location betrayal. A petabyte of zeros and ones every day. You and you and. Look at you. You deserve everything. You deserve everything you get.

:::: **APIS THE HEALER SONG**

Each man must assemble a memory palace within himself. Put one or two moments — never too few, never too many — in each room as you pass by. Let us say into this one, the one we currently inhabit, place your disgrace among the sweets in my bowl. In the next, rest on a shelf carved into the far wall Lady Tiresias' shrieks alongside the fragrance of your mother's breath. Farther, in the large chamber on your left, deposit a single majestic palm tree, its leaves mud-spattered with beliefs, and beside it your father, who clings to your back like a homunculus heavy as a handful of dried leaves.

Now burn that palace down.

:::: **PROFESSOR CELAN SOLEN SONG**

What I mean to suggest is that, while Descartes and
Leibniz both evinced lifelong alarm before the notion of
the maze, from Nietzsche forward philosophy — or, more
accurately, a certain developing counter- or un-philosophy
(Heidegger, Derrida, Deleuze and Guattari, et al.) —
embraced the maze's rhizomatic architecture for various
purposes: to picture the meandering pathways and blind
alleys of the human mind, to capture the trial-and-error
nature of thought, to fathom, perhaps —

:::: **DEBRIS**

— how King Cocalus summons Daedalus to unscramble Daddy's puzzle. The artificer ties a thin thread to an ant that strings the scarlet-mouthed Triton's trumpet as it goes. With that, Daddy demands the wretch be handed over for punishment for sneaking my sister the solution to my dilemma. Cocalus simpers, flounces, finally agrees, invites Daddy to enjoy an evening of festivities first: a feast featuring a wild boar stuffed with live thrushes, surrounded by pastry piglets suckling; a cake statue of Priapus, erection an oversized sweet roll dripping fresh cream. There will be wine-drinking contests, boxing, music, wrestling, poetry, races, and, to cap it all off, athletes somersaulting over the horns and backs of charging bulls. But before that: a ritual bath.

:::: APIS THE HEALER SONG

Because in the slick rust-gray entrails of a sacrificial goat I once divined there exist no monsters, only creatures appearing among us for the first time — and hence ones we are unable to recognize for what they are. These shocks to our lives should be treated as holy beings for which we do not yet possess a name.

They arrive to teach us how to unlearn everything we thought we once knew.

:::: **DEBRIS**

And so I watch him — watch Daddy — recline in the tub decorated with octopi and anemones, eyes half-lidded, raising a silver goblet to his lips.

Debris speaks into tomorrow shimmer.

Daddy remains time curtained.

:::: **DEBRIS**

And so I watch the dream stranger raise his mother's stiff hand to kiss the queen goodbye, bow before his wintry father's voice booming above him — watch a muscular young Chinese man traveling in a caravan along the Silk Road through the arid plains of Central Asia shoo a flea off his forearm — a middle-aged woman with abbreviated hair the color of deep space type the words 21 December 1972 on an orange Robotron manual with black keys.

:::: **DEBRIS**

Daddy convulses into a steam cloud, becoming a brief mention in the historians' chronicles.

:::: I LOVE YOU SONG

Because the traveler on the Silk Road is musing hazily about his wife back home as he walks beneath a fiery white sun, recalling how the fragrance of her breath spices the cool darkness when she nuzzles up against him at night. The carbon dioxide he exhales draws the flea into the long snaggled hair curling around his neck. The flea drills down and squirts saliva into the vein on which it begins feeding to prevent the traveler's blood from coagulating.

I am only the things that pass through me, the traveler thinks, wondering what he means.

:::: **DEBRIS**

Because six hundred years later, a short, flinty German with greasy hair, thumb-tip mustache, and uniform the color of pumice bends over the map stretched before him across a large wooden table to plan his invasion of my heart.

:::: SIR ARTHUR EVANS SONG

Because no matter on how many occasions we calculated the number of rooms, we invariably arrived at a different sum. I presume this misreckoning was due in greater part to how each man counting conceived the concept *room* — some being no larger than a wardrobe or privy, others the size of an immense banquet hall — than to any sorcery attributed to the site by the gullible locals.

:::: **DEBRIS**

Which, I suppose, begs the question: *How long have I been here?*

Surely one of the easiest to answer — assuming reliable definitions for such concepts as *long, be, I*, and *here*.

Another way of saying this: I watched a French soldier shit himself into the next life, fetaled in agony on a pallet in a hospital tent on a frozen field on the outskirts of Moscow, a surge of bloody mucus gobbing his pants.

Milkweed parachutes flustering the enamel-blue sky above my island adrift in a seascape of hammered go —

:::: APIS THE HEALER SONG

Daedalus built your heart, not from stone, but from a vast colony of tiny shapeshifting invertebrates that only resemble stone in look and feel.

I believe this is what has become of the dead.

:::: **DIODORUS SICULUS SONG**

For that reason some say Daedalus, visiting Egypt and admiring the skill shown in this colossal edifice, constructed for Minos, king of Crete, who died horribly at the hands of King Cocalus, a labyrinth like it, in which was kept, as the myth relates —

:::: **DEBRIS**

Does anyone —

:::: **NICK BOSTROM SONG**

So to come to the point of my talk this afternoon — and thank you again to the people at TED for inviting me to speak here at Oxford — at least one of the three propositions I've discussed must reasonably be the case:

:::: THE TERRIBLE ANGELS SONG

Jump and it's exemption all the way down.

:::: DIODORUS SICULUS SONG

— as the myth relates, a beast called Minotaur; yet, be
that as it may —

:::: JULIAN ASSANGE SONG

I never had a mentor, so I was forced to make myself up
as I went along.

:::: **DIODORUS SICULUS SONG**

— yet, be that as it may, the labyrinth in Crete has entirely disappeared, whether it be that some ruler razed it to the ground or that the years themselves have effaced the work, although the one in Egypt has stood intact in its entirety down to our lifetime and the composition of this, my universal history from the origin of the world to the present day.

:::: I LOVE YOU SONG

The flea springs from the traveler's neck to the shins of a tubby, short-winded man lumbering beside him. From there into the fine fur on the underbelly of a rat sleeping among barrels in a nearby supply cart.

Before long the caravan reaches the small fleet of merchant ships docked along the weatherworn Crimean coast. Several traders have already begun noticing freckly rashes around their fresh fleabites. Three feel softly dazed, no longer fully at home in this dimension. Fearful of their companions' reactions, they keep their strangenesses to themselves.

Over the next two years, the Black Death culls sixty percent of Europe's population.

lance olsen

:::: **POSEIDON CHORUS**

:::: **PROFESSOR CELAN SOLEN SONG**

Which is to say, as the director at the Bibliothèque Nationale in Buenos Aires submits for our consideration, *there are hours when Ariadne's thread is —*

:::: **DEBRIS**

A middle-aged woman with abbreviated hair the color of deep space and dark red cat-eye glasses types the words *21 December 1972* — types *Dear Ms. Sontag:* — on an orange Robotron manual with black keys shaped like rounded triangles.

:::: **DEBRIS**

— *broken, Button,* whispers Mommy out of the darkness, rocking.

:::: **PROFESSOR CELAN SOLEN SONG**

Nor should we forget Ariadne's ball of string is also known as a *clew*, phonetic variant of *clue*: namely, that which points the way for Theseus until, in our contemporary, he hears a *snick* behind him, senses abrupt slackness.

:::: DEBRIS

By that I mean hundreds of wide-winged cubes hang in a desert of silence 22,236 miles above the equator, receiving and transmitting torrents of data in a broadband network deployed by legions of cartoon rockets from legions of countries and companies.

A brume of white periods poised at the edge of luminous white-blueness.

:::: **LETTER FROM EAST BERLIN SONG**

Dear Ms. Sontag:

I am very happy to receive your note. Excuse me the answer, but my English is frightening. You are kind for your nice words on my book.

All I want now to do is finish the next — a novel called *Franziska Linkerhand* over a young architect whose ideas of innovation conflict with the city planning office's. I think by what the D.D.R. has became since the last decade.

The breast cancer however seems to have other ideas. I wish that I could write something more bright to you but the fog has arrived. The doctors say that he is moved from the breasts to the lungs to the backbone to the brain. My body is a contamination network become.

However the part which really scares me is —

:::: **PROFESSOR VEIT ERLMANN SONG**

— is the unusually important role the labyrinth played in the medieval musical imagination. Between the mid-fifteenth and the mid-seventeenth centuries, for instance, the melody of *L'homme armé* appeared in over forty sacred Masses. In *The Maze and the Warrior*, Craig Wright argues the lyrics about the eponymous Armed Man entering tumultuous battle in reality represent —

:::: DEBRIS

One naturally encounters staircases, too. Maybe I should mention this. Some I've passed, yet never investigated. Others I've explored for hours or centuries — these words, these words — ascending or descending in search of the search, bedding down on this landing, that one, yet never reaching something that feels like a there. Some bump their noses against dead ends after six steps. Others stray onto new levels and radiate into further radiations.

:::: **PROFESSOR VEIT ERLMANN SONG**

— the lyrics about the eponymous Armed Man entering
tumultuous battle in reality represent, not a reference to
St. Michael the Archangel leading God's armies against
Satan in the Book of Revelation, as some have advanced,
nor the arming for a new crusade against the Turks, but
rather a retelling of Theseus descending into combat with
the black beast. More recently that formation has been
invoked in music to signify complex harmonic and hence
ontological relationships. Consider Peter Maxwell Davies'
opera, *Missa super l'homme armé* (for speaker or singer — male
or female — and ensemble). The opening arrangement of
an anonymous fifteenth-century mass immediately fissures
into exaggerated expressive gestures, a crisis of aurality.
The consequence: an exceptional investigation, not into
the past per se, but into the problematics of historical
knowledge, although, it should be added —

:::: **LETTER FROM EAST BERLIN SONG**

— the part which really scares me is, that the mental abilities rot. I feel myself every day to become dumber from the day before. I forget myself, cannot follow conversations to find the words. I am standing all at once alone in the rooms without to know why. I think maybe someone should begin to pin little notes to my bluse.

I am sorry to bore you with my problems. It is difficult to be honest about death. There should be more interesting things to say when you are 39 years old. It is hard to imagine, that the world will make farther its daily clatter without me. I am certain although, that she will not notice one fewer writer.

Mit besten Grüßen,
Brigitte Reimann

:::: **DEBRIS**

And before and after that I watched a skinny pair of legs
flashing into the sea and vanishing while, back on shore,
a boy herding goats bent down to remove a pebble from
his sandal and missed the tiny white misinterpretation
taking place briefly somewhere far behind him. Watched
a wild-haired Norse berserker, mind made multiple by
mushroom phantoms, bring down his two-handed ax into
the skull of a cowering apprentice on the floor of the choir
where the boy had fled in search of refuge on the Holy
Island of Lindisfarne, in mid-prayer the apprentice's body
shuddering into a fetal of clay.

:::: **SIR ARTHUR EVANS SONG**

— although, it should be added, while Mackenzie kept admirably detailed daily records, serving as middleman between myself and the indigenes, I must confess that I found it incumbent upon me to warn my associate on more than one occasion about his drinking habits, and, following an especially disconcerting night having found him passed out blind-sozzled on a camp table as I made my way to my tent, was forced to dismiss him from his responsibilities, notwithstanding the some thirty years over the course of which we had worked profitably side by side. Red-faced and pugnacious, Dr. Mackenzie of course denied the allegations, and I was quite sorry to see him —

:::: **DEBRIS**

— speak silence into —

lance olsen

:::: **SIR ARTHUR EVANS SONG**

— quite sorry to see him depart. Mr. Fyfe promptly assumed Mr. Mackenzie's duties in addition to his own — altogether unselfishly — accomplishing both with laudable results, and enabling the excavation of Knossos to proceed apace, the bulk of our undertaking brought to conclusion within a mere two y —

:::: **DEBRIS**

— speak silence into —

lance olsen

:::: CATASTROPHE CHORUS

of mind

incest   ?

Why do monsters cease?

love?

:::: DEBRIS

I speak silence into my mouth.

:::: DENIS DIDEROT SONG

And if you have a little imagination; if you can feel; if sounds captivate your soul, you will see a man who wakes up in the middle of a labyrinth. Here he is, looking to the right and left for a way out. With hesitant steps he follows a path, possibly misleading, that opens before him. Here he is, lost again. He runs, he rests, he runs again. Bruised from his repeated tumbles, he arrives, looks around, and recognizes the place where he woke up. Another appellation for this tale: the movement in a sonata known as the development, which allows composers an opportunity to explore a wide range of keys, and, by doing so, stage an elaborate musical drama.

:::: **DEBRIS**

Or this: the dream stranger one morning stepping out
onto a sun-rushed beach — this morning — call it this
morning — and not another — my beach — call it
that — the port of Poros-Katsambas — at last — or not
quite yet — soon — and after a short — for all practical
— cautiously taking in his — what? — yes — soon —
cautiously taking in his new surroundings as he moves
among my other donations — wondering — listen — you
can — what? — yes — you can hear him wondering —

:::: THE TERRIBLE ANGELS SONG

You filthy —

:::: NICK BOSTROM SONG

At least one of the three propositions I've been discussing
must reasonably be the case:

> 1. the human species will go extinct before
> reaching a posthuman stage;
>
> 2. any posthuman civilization is extremely
> unlikely to be interested in —

:::: DEBRIS

— you can hear him wondering —

:::: THE TERRIBLE ANGELS SONG

You filthy little —

:::: DEBRIS

What I can tell you, I want to say, is your ancestors are burning.

:::: DEBRIS

— the sun-rushed beach — I thought we would never — what? — accompanied by my other guests — yes — and just like that — just like that all the —

lance olsen

:::: DEBRIS

:::: DEBRIS

— all the voices go away —

:::: DEBRIS

— the flutter lights blank out — sudden failings — access denied — flies in the head — straining to hear — *what?* — yes — but I forget the —

— where is —

— where is —

— where is everybody?

dreamlives of debris

:::: DEBRIS

lance olsen

:::: **DEBRIS**

Because Debris is —

:::: **DEBRIS**

Debris is afraid.

:::: **THE TERRIBLE ANGELS SONG**

You fucking retard. One step and —

:::: **DEBRIS**

We all have so much to carry, whispers Mommy out of the darkness, rocking.

:::: **DEBRIS**

And with that they return. The world stranges back into itself.

:::: **NICK BOSTROM SONG**

> 2. any posthuman civilization is extremely unlikely to be interested in or have overriding legal/moral restrictions against running simulations of their own historical biosphere wherein their forebears possess consciousness to the degree, say, that we do;

:::: **DEBRIS**

[[Will wonders never cease?]]

lance olsen

:::: **DEBRIS**

[[Will they never commence?]]

:::: MICHEL FOUCAULT SONG

And with that the Minotaur returns: the mythical expression of the very near and the very far. Of the very identity of words — by which I mean this simple, fundamental fact about language: there are fewer terms of designation than there are things to designate. The Minotaur epitomizes words as the unexpected meeting place of the most distant figures of reality, where distance itself is abolished. For language is a proliferation of distance, an extension of corridors that seem familiar and yet are always foreign.

Like a kiss.

The Minotaur performs the wealth of poverty called words, which always refer away from and lead back to themselves, lost and found and lost again forever.

:::: DEBRIS

Because the dream stranger raises his mother's stiff hand to kiss the queen goodbye, bows before his wintry father's voice booming above him, and then he is stepping past Ariadne busily competing for a love no one will receive to enter my —

:::: NICK BOSTROM SONG

    3. we are living in a computer simulation.

:::: DEBRIS

— to enter my heart — and in that moment I once more become the things that pass through me — nothing more or less — because —

:::: **PLUTARCH SONG**

— because the ship wherein Theseus returned from Crete possessed thirty oars and was preserved by his countrymen down even to the time of Demetrius Phalereus, that great Peripatetic who inspired the creation of the Mouseion, location of the Library of Alexandria.

The Athenians removed the old planks as they decayed, replaced them with new and stronger timber. And thus did this ship become an example of the following philosophical question of identity: *Does an object that has had all its components replaced remain fundamentally the same object?*

I shall henceforth refer to this problem as The Theseus Paradox.

:::: DEBRIS

By this I mean, staring out over the ocean's endless waste, frothing the water white with stroke upon stroke, the dream stranger tumbles into a reverie about his father's meeting with Pythia, the immortal Delphic oracle, who possessed long hair the color of deep space, skin the color of snowblindness, eyes the color of flayed deer.

Pythia crouched in her birdcage hung from a leafless tree at the entrance to the cave above the Castalian Springs.

What do I want? Aegeus asked.

And Pythia answered: *You want to beware of the one-sandaled man. He will gut you.*

And what do you want? asked Aegeus.

And Pythia answered: *I want to die.*

:::: **NICK BOSTROM SONG**

Because within the computer simulation, posthuman beings would eventually run their own simulations. It follows that one would eventually encounter a nested simulation — simulations buried within simulations. Logic tells us it would be unreasonable to count ourselves among the small minority of genuine organisms who, sooner or later, will be vastly outnumbered by reproductions. Nor would it necessarily be impossible for us to tell if we are inhabiting one. A pop-up window could appear before us at any moment — as we are driving to work, brushing our teeth — announcing: *You are living in a simulation. Click here for more information.* Imperfections in a counterfeit environment could be difficult for native inhabitants to detect. Memory of a revelation might be purged, or treated by the culture as evidence of a nightmare, vision, or descent into madness.

:::: **APIS THE HEALER SONG**

Because your sister Ariadne is a trance of air. Her syntax error will poison you into ragged garments of behavior. Soon a plague of forgetfulness will break out among our people. Their recollections will become too full and harden into flakes of bark. Their mouth static will solidify, disarray from their lips, clack onto the stones around their feet as if th —

:::: **DEBRIS**

And with that Apis' head becomes breeze.

:::: **DEBRIS**

A great double-headed ax flickering.

:::: **DEBRIS**

I blink, trying to see what I am seeing, and then Apis' torso collapses into itself and his head clunks against a far wall, eyes half-lidding the ceiling. Behind the fierce bankruptcy of him stands Mommy in the doorway, smiling, beside her a hull-chested dispenser who must duck because this room is so crammed with him. *Some people love to hear themselves talk*, Mommy says, *don't they, Button? Some people just put too much faith in grammar.*

lance olsen

:::: BULL OF HEAVEN CHORUS

dreamlives of debris

:::: **ROBERT FAGLES SONG**

Because it is inevitable in such a process, with writing a newly acquired skill and its materials — papyrus or leather — not convenient for cross-reference, and with the epic composition itself appearing to have been "Homer's" lifework, that the final version of his text should contain a good many inconsistencies. Case in point: no one has ever, in spite of repeated and ingenious efforts, been able to produce a convincing ground plan for the palace of Odysseus; people enter and emerge from rooms that seem to shift position from one episode to the —

:::: DEBRIS

— next Daddy stands at the head of the royal cortege, awaiting my guests, ready to welcome them with music and wine and a bellowing of albino dwarfs, and — no — not that — that was something else — that was some other disappointment in the —

:::: **SLAVOJ ŽIŽEK SONG**

— the winding mountainous roads, the hotel corridors of illogic, the hedge maze itself, viewers sink ever deeper into the labyrinthine mystery of Kubrick's *The Shining*. And what do they find at its center? An insane man stalking his own child, the Minotaur its victim, Jack Danny, their family name — *Torrence* — echoing the Latin present participle: *torrens* — *burning, seething,* an expression of a violent rupture. Derrida notes: *The function of a center was not only to orient, balance, and organize the structure — one cannot in fact conceive of an unorganized structure — but above all to make sure that the organizing principle of the structure would limit what we might call the play of the structure. Even today the notion of a structure lacking any center represents the unthinkable itself.*

:::: **DEBRIS**

Look: the procession is migrating from port to palace. Daddy parades my visitors up the grand stone ramp flanked by tapering black columns whose caps are ringed with cinnabar bands. Leads them into the courtyard, beneath the great wooden lintels, into the main hall slabbed with olive schist, walled with icy gypsum, lined with man-sized alabaster vases, giant scarabs, and gigantic gold-wrapped elephant tusks, thinking as he goes —

:::: **SLAVOJ ŽIŽEK SONG**

Kubrick's 1980 translation of Stephen King's 1977 novel represents the house that Jacques un-built: its architecture argues we have lost our shared belief in a single unifying force. Our response has been to construct another Other in order to escape the intolerable freedom we face. A structure without a center is unimaginable, and thus we simulate its opposite, even if, as here, that center in the end is nothing short of pure insanity, the unconditional annihilation of innocence. To further echo Derrida: *Let us space.*

:::: **DEBRIS**

— thinking —

lance olsen

:::: MINOS CHORUS

:::: JOURNEY-FROM-ASS-TO-SOUL SONG

BERLIN (AP) — Since its inception in April 2011, the überhip electrodisco Salon Zur Wilden Renate's mystifying indoor labyrinth has become the stuff of this city's myth. The multi-room, multi-floor interzone known for its charming shabbiness and chilled crowds is housed in an unrenovated apartment building in Friedrichshain that seems a little different every time you enter. Ten euros and —

:::: **DEBRIS**

— and a banquet salutes them. Everyone understands it will be my guests' last. Female servants kneel to wash and oil their hands. An underfed bard with anguish-gray beard recites stories, all of them mistaken. The albino dwarfs carry in clay platters hilled with bread, tureens aslosh with shellfish stew, plates tiered with grilled pink sea bream, trays wealthed with tomatoes and green peppers and cucumbers and olives, with feta cheese and apples and honeydew and figs.

Afterward, Daddy ushers them into the shrine rooms to pray to the griffin and blue-green snake noise.

:::: **DEBRA'S MOTHER'S SONG**

Because my daughter's fallen in love with data. Like all she does all night is lay in bed playing The Theseus Paradox. What's homework? What's friends? And Nico? Useless per usual. Over his shoulder on the way out the door to meet his buds for a beer he says: *She's your daughter, hon.* Thanks for the fucking newsflash. And now? Now the game's all messed up. Debra trundles downstairs shouting: *The walls just killed me! They're not supposed to do that. I just ATE him and he's BACK again. That's totally UNFAIR.* I ask her if she's read the instructions and she just like stands there, staring at me, face one hundred percent devoid of muscles. *Call tech support*, she says. *NOW*.

:::: **DEBRIS**

Because before and after that I watch Ariadne standing
regally beside my daddy — eyes for the first time falling
on the dream stranger — his right foot lowering onto the
warm sand — his left — stepping with my other guests
from the galley into afterlife — watch how Ariadne's
thoughts chaos with pity — her earth becoming somebody
else's — no longer knowing what a tree is — how at the
banquet that evening she burgles a few words with him —
wishes him good fortune — how later she slips out a side
door into the cricketing night to search for the key to the
treasure and —

:::: **DEBRIS**

She finds it. Doesn't. Her name comes to mean   .
Comes to mean

                              . She marries Dionysus. No.
Theseus. She helps him because

                              . He tricks her into
it. She's too young to know any better. Her father is brutal.
She wants   . She wants —

:::: **PROFESSOR COLLEEN NAS SONG**

One of the largest volcanic events in recorded history, the Thera eruption was four to five times more powerful than the Krakatoan, exploding with the nearly incomprehensible energy of several hundred atomic bombs. In a fraction of a second, the political landscape of the ancient world changed. That blast caused turmoil in Egypt. Its environmental effects could be felt as far away as North America. Many believe it inspired Plato's myth of Atlantis in *Timaeus*. Its effects have been cited to explain such Old Testament plagues as the days of darkness and the polluting of the rivers. Moreover —

:::: JOURNEY-FROM-ASS-TO-SOUL SONG

— a quiet word to the bar staff leads to a gold coin and magical cupboard. Your guide shuts the door behind you and you feel deeply on your own.

"It's not simply a maze," co-founder Georg Losch explains emphatically. "That's why so many people freak out. It's a journey from your ass to your soul."

Behind the cupboard you find—

:::: **DEBRIS**

She finds it. Doesn't. Longs to leave her life on Crete
behind because Dionysus, who beats her every

                            . No. Theseus' coppery eyes. His rippled
abdomen. Because after their getaway a storm. Pregnant
Ariadne put ashore on Naxos, Theseus swept out to —
No. Because he — Who? Because Theseus abandons her
while she sleeps. Or Dionysus

                                        . And so
she hangs herself from a leafless tree. Dies in childbirth.
Remains faithful to   . Remains unfaithful to —
No. Learns to love her father a little more with each —

:::: **JOURNEY-FROM-ASS-TO-SOUL SONG**

— you find yourself in cramped quarters imagined in equal parts by David Lynch and Werner Herzog. A psychedelic soundscape escorts you on your climb, slide and crawl through a sinuous digestive tract of narrow tunnels, vaginas, rectums and wombs lined with unknown specimens.

By the time you reach the lower depths of dungeons and perpetual darkness, you may have realized —

:::: **DEBRIS**

— with each passing slap. Marries no one because early one morning Perseus in a rage flings a spear at Theseus, who ducks, flings a spear at Dionysus, who ducks, and pierces Ariadne's throat. Her teeth-shattered mouth. Blood pouring out onto the warm sand. She breathes love as she dies. Because — No. Zeus makes her deathless. Jealous Artemis, guardian of young girls, noise of diseases, drowns her, stones her, knifes her, tears her to pieces on the shady banks of a brook like a cat a shocked curlew.

And Ariadne lives happily ever after, lying lost and dying in the hallways of my problem, strangling on her own thread.

:::: DEBRIS

Or an orange sunrise. Daddy piloting my ephemera down through the tight workshop lanes, craftsmen already busy chipping stone, throwing clay, smelting bronze. Past the wheat and oil storage magazines, through an olive grove, to the base of a hill, that hill, this, the morning cobwebby with pearled light, and —

:::: DEBRIS

— and then they are standing before the gate I could not place —

:::: DEBRIS

— we are standing before the gate I could not place —

:::: DEBRIS

— saying —

:::: DEBRIS

— they are saying —

:::: DEBRA'S SONG

— it doesn't WORK keeps changing crashing starting over everything happening at once and there are all these VOICES and PHONE TECH SUPPORT do it call do it call do it DOOOOOOOOO IIIIIIIIIIIIIIIIIIIIIIIIIIIIT —

:::: **JOURNEY-FROM-ASS-TO-SOUL SONG**

— you may have realized this is one rabbit hole you didn't want to go down. Yet in this Bizarro World According to Dr. Losch, it's all about how you approach the journey.

"Some people go through it like they go through life," he says. "They look for an exit. Others give themselves over completely in celebration of the holy mess called being awake."

:::: **DEBRIS**

Ariadne senses herself coming awake as she slips out the side door into the cricketing night.

They find each other, find a dark nook among the royal apartments, embrace.

Kiss.

Theseus' chapped hands reach for her fifteen-year-old breasts.

Cheeks hot, chest flurrying, Ariadne lowers herself to her knees on the cool olive schist, fingers grabbling under the prince's loincloth, remembering what the nurses taught her about what to do, and —

:::: **DEBRIS**

— and a priestess steps from the procession, bronze dagger raised toward belief.

In my mirror world, I lift Catastrophe.

Slaves steady the slow-lowing bull ruffling with sacrificial ribbons, and —

:::: **PLATO SONG**

— and afterwards there occurred violent earthquakes and floods; and in a single day and night of misfortune all your warlike men in a body sank into the earth, and the island of Atlantis in like manner disappeared into the depths of the sea —

:::: DEBRIS

— because the dream stranger bows before his wintry father whose voice booms above him, saying: *Your vessel will depart with a black sail. I have given the captain a white one as well. Should the noises smile upon us, he will hoist the latter upon his return. Beholding that sail, the people of Athens will know this is what victory feels like. But should the noises' curse abide, the captain will hoist the black, and then our people will know their children will return to them no more.*

:::: **DEBRIS**

Shocked, Ariadne slaps him across the startled face.

Tries to slap him, but the prince snatches her wrist midflight.

Squeezes with his massive hand.

Harder.

You're hurting me, she hisses, eyes tearing with fury and fright. *Stop. Stop it. Let g* —

:::: **DEBRIS**

And does she find it? Does she long to leave her life on
Crete? There are spears. Are his eyes really copper or
rather blue or green, gray or black? Where does the storm
come from? How many bewilder to life in Ariadne's belly?
There are metaphors and there are — What? Is the last
sound the prince hears demon laughter or his own lungs
failing with water? And her eyes. Are they open as her
body dangles from that tree, or closed as she lies in the
hallways of my nonsense, remaining forever faithful to —
forever unfaithful to —

lance olsen

:::: **DEBRIS**

[[There are theories the color of dandelions.]]

:::: **DEBRIS**

— the bloody waterfall spilling from the collection bowl over the priestess' head, shoulders, bare breasts. Unhurriedly she smears her face and neck, sucks the rusty wetness from her fingers. And behind this scene, another: the dirty white plume rising into the orange sky where the island of Thera floats just beyond our view like a northern emergency.

:::: APIS THE HEALER SONG

Because the day will come and has come when the citizens of our kingdom awoke unable to remember where they had locked their gold earrings and love. Dazed, unsure which foot to slip into which sandal, they dressed and one by one discovered themselves trickling into the market square. They avoided their friends as if those friends were foreigners, noises having looted each of their names.

When they opened their mouths to speak, all they heard was their own wordbark ticking onto the stones below.

They stared down, faces devoid of muscles, bewildered at the bone-white sound garbage.

:::: **DEBRIS**

— and I am running again — yes — bolting not too strong a word — bolting through corridors shaking themselves to pieces around me — stones smashing down like conclusions — dust like fog — this world in an act of unthinking — *what?* — yes — this — the great convulsion — let us call it that — the rapid same silversheen questions — this — *what?* — yes — we are racing through the clauses of — herself — arms raised high above my head — crying out: *Help me! Help me! Please, somebody: Help me!* — realizing as water sluices over your ankles sometimes it is too late to change — this idea the only one left you — sluices over your shins — forcing Debris to grub out the next staircase and scramble up — and the next after that — a runnel — a rush —

:::: THE TERRIBLE ANGELS SONG

Look at you. You and you and you. Do it. Come on. Do it.

:::: DEBRIS

— because Debris is —

:::: ARIADNE SONG

— just my hand on his thigh, just there, just like that, look, just my fingers moving beneath his loincloth, just the tips, the slowness of them, the heat of his skin, just —

:::: DEBRIS

— Debris is —

:::: **DEBRIS**

Or I could tell you a different story. Maybe the one about how Ariadne sensed herself coming awake as she slipped from the banquet out the side door into the cricketing night, how in a dark nook among the royal apartments she stumbled upon Dionysus on his knees, fingers grabbling under Theseus' loi —

:::: **DEBRIS**

Not darkness. Sunset. Sunrise. It is difficult to tell which. The one about the dirty white plume churning up like an exclamation on the horizon hours before the first tremors arrive. The slaves steadying the slow-lowing bull ruffling with sacrificial ribbons, and in a single gesture the priestess steps forward and claws her bronze dagger across its pulsing throat. The massive bull flinches, shudders, drops to its knees, and there, off to the side: the prince watching Ariadne reaching for the slight bunching beneath her robes.

The treasure passing hands.

:::: **APIS THE HEALER SONG**

Because the day will come and has come when the citizens of our kingdom forgot how to organize their houses and then their lives. Pottery shards collected in the lanes among piles of shredded straw and crushed seashells and lifeless pets and bent brooches and goat femurs. People began to remember strangers' childhoods as their own. The sensation was like a difficult philosophy, a yellow-blue evening sky.

:::: **DEBRIS**

And I bewilder into consciousness, snapping, Mommy stroking my head as she slides Catastrophe out of my arms.

There, there, Button, she whispers. *Go back to sleep.*

I try sitting up to retrieve my brother but Mommy presses a sweetness rag over my nose and mouth. All I can do is watch as before and after that she delivers him to a priest standing in a small shrine in a large cave atop a stony mountain. The priest accepts her offering and gently goes about the task of breaking my brother's arms, his legs, his back in order to truss him into an embryonic curl for burial because —

Because —

:::: **DEBRIS**

Because it is Dionysus on his knees in that dark nook among the royal apartments, head bobbing beneath the prince's loincloth.

Shocked, Ariadne steps forward and slaps the prince across his startled face. Tries to slap him. Theseus snatches her wrist midflight, squeezes, demanding:

Who are *you?* What are you *doing* here?

You're *hurting* me, she hisses, eyes flaring. *Stop. Stop it. Let go!*

But Dionysus is already on his feet, already behind her, fingers around her neck.

The only thought convening inside the noise's head the need to keep her still, encourage all the sounds of her to go away.

:::: **APIS THE HEALER SONG**

Because the day will come and has come when the
citizens of our kingdom began to regard their spouses as
imposters sent by enemies to undo them. They slept in
separate rooms, bolts thrown, disbelieving everything their
husbands or wives said. Refused to eat at the same table
for fear of winter. And soon they began to rise from their
toilets having forgotten to wipe with the vinegar-soaked
sponge in the clay bowl by their feet. Meandered through
the alleys and across the market square, loincloths hiked
up absentmindedly around their hips, piss-shit trickling
down the backs of their legs.

We refer to this period as The Age of Water's Afterlife.

:::: DEBRIS

In the cave atop the mountain the priest lowered trussed Catastrophe into a terracotta pithos decorated with dolphins to help swim my brother from this logic error to the next. The priest sealed the jar with a disinterested kiss, the cave with nobody prayers.

This is the story about how Brother became a new tense.

:::: **DEBRIS**

Before and after that I watch myselves closing in from behind on my next donation. She's taller than most, hair long and abundant black. She wears a white sacrificial tunic over which drapes a purple shawl adorned with detailed geometric designs. She hears my feet chafing as I make my final advance. Sensing the density of my companionship, she turns and I see his coppery eyes and come up short.

In a single gesture he swipes off the black wig, draws my sister's bronze affection from beneath his shawl.

:::: DEBRIS

— and before and after that I watched him — his
companions — Love Amnesia skimming through their
bloodstreams — watched them in their joy forget to
change black sail to white as their king had commanded
— watched Aegeus watch for their return from his position
high atop the ragged white cliff — his face harden as he
catches sight of the galley scudding into view — a certain
thought gathering like a blizzard behind his forehead —
watched as he simply takes four deliberate steps toward
the edge of the cliff — then one more — the field of
wave-frothed rocks hurling to receive him — his own
son his own murderer — somewhere the Delphic oracle
crouched in her birdcage in that leafless tree — flayed-
deer eyes squinting — a grin —

:::: **DEBRIS**

Let her go! commands the prince.

I — I — I — Dionysus stammers, eyes swelling with fury and fright, Ariadne's body crumpling out from under him. *I just wanted to —*

Twine pinched around her purpling neck.

:::: **DEBRIS**

All seconds, it strikes me, collect into this second.

:::: **DEBRIS**

All seconds into —

:::: **PROFESSOR COLLEEN NAS SONG**

The earthquakes and tsunami the eruption generated sometime between 1645 B.C. and 1500 B.C. devastated Minoan coastal settlements, first through fire, then through flood. The blast, heard three thousand miles away, killed forty thousand people within the first few hours and dropped global temperatures by several degrees. Curiously colored sunsets distracted the sky for three years.

:::: **DEBRIS**

I gently lowered myselves to our knees on the cold floor and raised my arms.

:::: **DEBRIS**

Ariadne's face fluxes into slackness, shit-piss reek wafting up around her. And all at once she is no longer looking at them, the prince, the noise, but at belief beyond through half-lidded eyes.

:::: **DEBRIS**

And behind this scene, another: the clamor of soldiers tumbling up the staircase.

:::: **DEBRIS**

Because I bewilder into consciousness, snapping, to discover Daedalus massaging my shoulder. His rumpled gray face floats in front of mine. His stooped, skinny son holds two large gray-white planks behind him. No. Not — Smoke fogs the air, my heart on fire everywhere.

It's time, he whispers. *Come.*

:::: **DEBRIS**

Because three minutes earlier, at the banquet, Pasiphaë raises her head, listening to the far side of listening.

That sound, she asks no one. *What is th* —

:::: **ARIADNE SONG**

— *just the soft bump against the head of his swollen cock, the sweet sea-salt tang of precum on the tip of my tongue, just that and nothing else, just all these seconds collecting into this second, just the way he smells, saffron, sweat, sun, just these and nothing more, just here, just like this, just my right hand moving —*

:::: DEBRIS

A simple orange malignity stretched above us. Let's call it sunset. Sunrise. Daedalus, Icarus, and I stand before the gate I couldn't place until now. But it isn't the sky that overwhelms me. It is the ocean of precise smells — dense, sharp, as if I am reborn second by second, each a rupture, a rapture: grilling goat, acrid wine, rotting feet, alarming smoke, rabbit stew, baking bread, chipping stone, bitter barley, spoiling vegetables, sour bodies, woody frankincense, dirty wool, sticky figs, churned-up dust in the gusted-up air, and our palace is burning down.

:::: DEBRIS

Somewhere within the fumbling dark Theseus is sure he slipped it in, yes, the long groan, hot wetness, the indescribable newness of it, and smiling to himself he decides he will do this thing, and then he will do the other, and —

:::: **DEBRIS**

— and they lead me through the flooding difficulties of my problem — I become our eyes — Daedalus our map — all those wall scratchings having — *what?* — yes — all those wall scratchings perhaps having paid off — yet we travel for hours — *what?* — no — these words, these — *what?* — yes — smoke thickening — breathing an assignment — cold seawater rising over my shins — my — *what?* — no — and rounding a corner — it's as easy as — *what?* — yes — rounding a corner we step out of nightness into a warfare of sun.

:::: **DEBRIS**

Debris goes deaf.

:::: **DEBRIS**

Debris goes blind.

:::: **DEBRIS**

Debris stalls, idling, to take in the rapture ocean, and —

:::: **DEBRIS**

Black cinders sifting down around us.

Warm palm on my head, Daedalus explains: *You kept us alive. Now it's our turn.*

Behind him Icarus cradles an extra pair of wings built from rat hair, sacrificial tunics, bones, wax, and hope for Mommy's Little Duration.

Here, he says. *Put these on.*

:::: **DEBRIS**

— and Ariadne, unmoving, stares at them from the floor through half-lidded eyes as the shouts tumble up the staircase. Panicked, Theseus slaps her, trying to appall her awake. Nothing lucks. Again, harder, and her mouth falls open. A third time, sharp and quick, and my sister vexes into cough, bloody necklace looping her throat.

The first bangs arrive on the door. The ground begins to shiver.

:::: **DEBRIS**

And Daedalus is speaking and Icarus speaking and the artificer is helping his son on with his wings —

:::: **DEBRIS**

— saying —

:::: **ARIADNE SONG**

— and just the soft bump against the head of his swollen cock, how in my mouth it becomes the world, just that and nothing else, just that and his immense hand on the back of my head, just these things, the tightness in the pit of my tummy, his fingers in my hair, just the way he tugs it, just a little, just these and nothing more, just here, just like this, just like my nurses taught me, just the nightness behind my forehead crackling —

:::: **DEBRIS**

— and the door bursts open. Swords drawn, soldiers pour in to discover an empty. No. Ariadne lying motionless. No. The princess noisily riding   . Columns shaking themselves apart.   Because she has never.   Because she is lying motionless on the.   Because her name will come to mean

                        . Her lover glances over her head at the. Her father, clinging to her back like a homunculus heavy as a handful of dried leaves,

                                        . Or how she tightens the rope around her own neck, kicks the stool out from under her in a damp rocky field, and in that last breath uselessly changes her mind.

:::: **DEBRIS**

Rocking, Mommy whispers out of the darkness: *You are living in a simulation, Button. Click here for more information.*

:::: **DEBRIS**

And behind this scene, another: the clamor of soldiers, swords drawn, tumbling up the hill toward us because when Daedalus' palm touches my head I secretly lean into it and all the screamings break off.

:::: **DEBRIS**

All the seconds —

:::: DEBRIS

Be careful, Daedalus explains. Icarus kneels behind me, tightening my straps. *Remember: don't fly too low lest your wings touch waves, nor too high lest the sun melt the wax binding the rat hairs tog —*

And then the soldiers are upon us.

:::: DEBRIS

Jump! Daedalus cries. *Now! Catch the air!*

:::: THE TERRIBLE ANGELS SONG

Go ahead, you pitiful fuck. Jump. Do it. One step and —

:::: **DEBRIS**

— and a warm black-flecked gust hooks his own huge wings and the pasty man-sized toad jerks off the ground.

:::: **DEBRIS**

Eight inches.

 Five feet.

 His son's body stirs, lifts beside him.

:::: **DEBRIS**

Rising, father and son seem surprised by physics.

lance olsen

:::: THE TERRIBLE ANGELS SONG

What are you waiting for? You got what you wanted. Do it. Go ahead. Do it. Do it do it do it do it do it —

:::: DEBRIS

The soldier at the front of the squad catches sight of me. Then, one by one, the others. Their eyes remodel into disbelief.

If this is nature, their expressions say, *blot it out.*

:::: DEBRIS

But Debris doesn't jump.

:::: DEBRIS

She can't.

:::: DEBRIS

She falters, wondering —

:::: **DEBRIS**

— wondering —

:::: **DEBRIS**

Where is everybody?

:::: DEBRIS

Debris can't move because Debris can't hear.

The soldiers rush at her and, looking up at Daedalus and Icarus shrinking into the sooting accident air, she waits.

:::: DEBRIS

Father and son hang against the orange sunball like dragonflies hanging.

Haltingly, they pivot toward the sea.

:::: DEBRIS

The sky gradually becomes garbled language. Her best friends gradually become somewhere elsc.

lance olsen

:::: **DEBRIS**

A lungful of sadness before the soldiers' hatred reaches her, Debris turns and slips back into her unburning, unflooding heart, wings trailing behind her.

:::: **DEBRIS**

Ten steps, and the screamings resume.

Twenty, and peace settles on her like the memory of Daedalus' palm.

:::: **DEBRIS**

Stilling, stilling, something catches my eye. An otherness in my surroundings: the white twine line fading forward into darkness, one end tied around a large stone by my feet.

:::: DEBRIS

I squat, raise it, snip the thread with my restless teeth, stand, and begin to follow, curious to see where it leads, what new toy lies at the —